Catwings

Ursula K. Le Guin

A CATWINGS TALE

Catwings

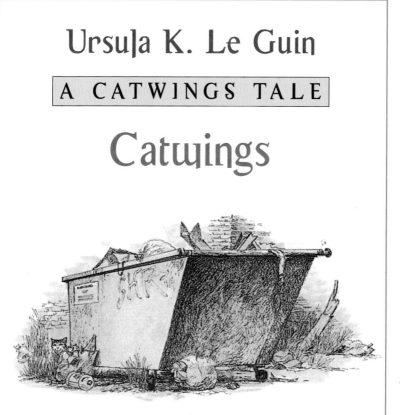

Illustrations by

S. D. SCHINDLER

ORCHARD BOOKS • NEW YORK

An Imprint of Scholastic Inc.

ISBN-13: 978-0-439-55189-2
ISBN-10: 0-439-55189-7

20 19 18 17 16   15 16 17 18/0

Printed in the U.S.A.   40

This Orchard paperback edition, October 2006

The text of this book is set in 14 point CG Cloister.
The illustrations are pen-and-ink drawings and wash.

7292

To all the cats I've loved before

—U. K. Le G.

Catwings

CHAPTER 1

MRS. JANE TABBY could not explain why all four of her children had wings.

"I suppose their father was a fly-by-night," a neighbor said, and laughed unpleasantly, sneaking round the dumpster.

"Maybe they have wings because I dreamed, before they were born, that I could fly away from this neighborhood," said Mrs. Jane Tabby. "Thelma, your face is dirty; wash it. Roger, stop hitting James. Harriet, when you purr, you should close your eyes part way and knead me with your front paws; yes, that's the way. How is the milk this morning, children?"

"It's very good, Mother, thank you," they answered happily. They were beautiful

children, well brought up. But Mrs. Tabby worried about them secretly. It really was a terrible neighborhood, and getting worse. Car wheels and truck wheels rolling past all day —rubbish and litter—hungry dogs—endless shoes and boots walking, running, stamping, kicking—nowhere safe and quiet, and less and less to eat. Most of the sparrows had moved away. The rats were fierce and dangerous; the mice were shy and scrawny.

So the children's wings were the least of Mrs. Tabby's worries. She washed those silky wings every day, along with chins and paws and tails, and wondered about them now and then, but she worked too hard finding food and bringing up the family to think much about things she didn't understand.

But when the huge dog chased little Harriet and cornered her behind the garbage

can, lunging at her with open, white-toothed
jaws, and Harriet with one desperate mew flew
straight up into the air and over the dog's
staring head and lighted on a rooftop—then
Mrs. Tabby understood.

The dog went off growling, its tail between its legs.

"Come down now, Harriet," her mother called. "Children, come here please, all of you."

They all came back to the dumpster. Harriet was still trembling. The others all purred with her till she was calm, and then Mrs. Jane Tabby said: "Children, I dreamed a dream before you were born, and I see now what it meant. This is not a good place to grow up in, and you have wings to fly from it. I want you to do that. I know you've been practicing. I saw James flying across the alley last night —and yes, I saw you doing nose dives, too, Roger. I think you are ready. I want you to have a good dinner and fly away—far away."

"But Mother—" said Thelma, and burst into tears.

"I have no wish to leave," said Mrs. Tabby

quietly. "My work is here. Mr. Tom Jones proposed to me last night, and I intend to accept him. I don't want you children underfoot!"

All the children wept, but they knew that that is the way it must be, in cat families. They were proud, too, that their mother trusted them to look after themselves. So all together they had a good dinner from the garbage can that the dog had knocked over. Then Thelma, Roger, James, and Harriet purred goodbye to their dear mother, and one after another they spread their wings and flew up, over the alley, over the roofs, away.

Mrs. Jane Tabby watched them. Her heart was full of fear and pride.

"They are remarkable children, Jane," said Mr. Tom Jones in his soft, deep voice.

"Ours will be remarkable too, Tom," said Mrs. Tabby.

CHAPTER 2

AS THELMA, Roger, James, and Harriet flew on, all they could see beneath them, mile after mile, was the city's roofs, the city's streets.

A pigeon came swooping up to join them. It flew along with them, peering at them uneasily from its little, round, red eye. "What kind of birds are you, anyways?" it finally asked.

"Passenger pigeons," James said promptly.

Harriet mewed with laughter.

The pigeon jumped in mid-air, stared at her, and then turned and swooped away from them in a great, quick curve.

"I wish I could fly like that," said Roger.

"Pigeons are really dumb," James muttered.

"But my wings ache already," Roger said, and Thelma said, "So do mine. Let's land somewhere and rest."

Little Harriet was already heading down towards a church steeple.

They clung to the carvings on the church roof, and got a drink of water from the roof gutters.

"Sitting in the catbird seat!" sang Harriet, perched on a pinnacle.

"It looks different over there," said Thelma, pointing her nose to the west. "It looks softer."

They all gazed earnestly westward, but cats don't see the distance clearly.

"Well, if it's different, let's try it," said James, and they set off again. They could not fly with untiring ease, like the pigeons. Mrs.

Tabby had always seen to it that they ate well, and so they were quite plump, and had to beat their wings hard to keep their weight aloft. They learned how to glide, not beating their wings, letting the wind bear them up; but Harriet found gliding difficult, and wobbled badly.

After another hour or so they landed on the roof of a huge factory, even though the air there smelled terrible, and there they slept for a while in a weary, furry heap. Then, towards

nightfall, very hungry—for nothing gives an appetite like flying—they woke and flew on.

The sun set. The city lights came on, long strings and chains of lights below them, stretching out towards darkness. Towards darkness they flew, and at last, when around them and under them everything was dark except for one light twinkling over the hill, they descended slowly from the air and landed on the ground.

A soft ground—a strange ground! The only ground they knew was pavement, asphalt, cement. This was all new to them, dirt, earth, dead leaves, grass, twigs, mushrooms, worms. It all smelled extremely interesting. A little creek ran nearby. They heard the song of it and went to drink, for they were very thirsty. After drinking, Roger stayed crouching on the bank, his nose almost in the water, his eyes gazing.

"What's that in the water?" he whispered.

The others came and gazed. They could just make out something moving in the water, in the starlight—a silvery flicker, a gleam. Roger's paw shot out....

"I think it's dinner," he said.

After dinner, they curled up together again under a bush and fell asleep. But first Thelma, then Roger, then James, and then small Harriet, would lift their head, open an eye, listen a moment, on guard. They knew they had come to a much better place than the alley, but they also knew that every place is dangerous, whether you are a fish, or a cat, or even a cat with wings.

CHAPTER 3

"IT'S ABSOLUTELY unfair," the thrush cried.

"Unjust!" the finch agreed.

"Intolerable!" yelled the bluejay.

"I don't see why," a mouse said. "You've always had wings. Now they do. What's unfair about that?"

The fish in the creek said nothing. Fish never do. Few people know what fish think about injustice, or anything else.

"I was bringing a twig to the nest just this morning, and a *cat* flew down, a cat *flew* down, from the top of the Home Oak, and *grinned* at me in mid-air!" the thrush said, and all the other songbirds cried, "Shocking! Unheard of! Not allowed!"

"You could try tunnels," said the mouse, and trotted off.

The birds had to learn to get along with the Flying Tabbies. Most of the birds, in fact, were more frightened and outraged than really endangered, since they were far better flyers than Roger, Thelma, Harriet, and James. The birds never got their wings tangled up in pine branches and never absent-mindedly bumped into tree trunks, and when pursued they could escape by speeding up or taking evasive action. But they were alarmed, and with good cause, about their fledglings. Many birds had eggs in the nest now; when the babies hatched, how could they be kept safe from a cat who could fly up and perch on the slenderest branch, among the thickest leaves?

It took a while for the Owl to understand this. Owl is not a quick thinker. She is a long thinker. It was late in spring, one evening, when she was gazing fondly at her two new owlets, that she saw James flitting by, chasing bats. And she slowly thought, "This will not do...."

And softly Owl spread her great, gray wings, and silently flew after James, her talons opening.

THE FLYING TABBIES had made their nest in a hole halfway up a big elm, above fox and coyote level and too small for raccoons to get into. Thelma and Harriet were washing each other's necks and talking over the day's adventures when they heard a pitiful crying at the foot of the tree.

"James!" cried Harriet.

He was crouching under the bushes, all scratched and bleeding, and one of his wings dragged upon the ground.

"It was the Owl," he said, when his sisters had helped him climb painfully up the tree trunk to their home hole. "I just escaped. She caught me, but I scratched her, and she let go for a moment."

And just then Roger came scrambling into the nest with his eyes round and black and full of fear. "She's after me!" he cried. "The Owl!"

They all washed James's wounds till he fell asleep.

"Now we know how the little birds feel," said Thelma, grimly.

"What will James do?" Harriet whispered. "Will he ever fly again?"

"He'd better not," said a soft, large voice just outside their door. The Owl was sitting there.

The Tabbies looked at one another. They did not say a word till morning came.

At sunrise Thelma peered cautiously out. The Owl was gone. "Until this evening," said Thelma.

From then on they had to hunt in the daytime and hide in their nest all night; for the Owl thinks slowly, but the Owl thinks long.

James was ill for days and could not hunt at all. When he recovered, he was very thin and could not fly much, for his left wing soon grew stiff and lame. He never complained. He sat for hours by the creek, his wings folded, fishing. The fish did not complain either. They never do.

One night of early summer the Tabbies were all curled in their home hole, rather tired and discouraged. A raccoon family was quarreling loudly in the next tree. Thelma had found nothing to eat all day but a shrew, which gave her indigestion. A coyote had chased Roger away from the wood rat he had been about to catch that afternoon. James's fishing had been unsuccessful. The Owl kept flying past on silent wings, saying nothing.

Two young male raccoons in the next tree started a fight, cursing and shouting insults. The other raccoons all joined in, screeching and scratching and swearing.

"It sounds just like the old alley," James remarked.

"Do you remember the Shoes?" Harriet asked dreamily. She was looking quite plump, perhaps because she was so small. Her sister and brothers had become thin and rather scruffy.

"Yes," James said. "Some of them chased me once."

"Do you remember the Hands?" Roger asked.

"Yes," Thelma said. "Some of them picked me up once. When I was just a kitten."

"What did they do—the Hands?" Harriet asked.

"They squeezed me. It hurt. And the hands person was shouting—'Wings! Wings! It has wings!'—that's what it kept shouting in its silly voice. And squeezing me."

"What did you do?"

"I bit it," Thelma said, with modest pride. "I bit it, and it dropped me, and I ran back to

Mother, under the dumpster. I didn't know how to fly yet."

"I saw one today," said Harriet.

"What? A Hands? A Shoes?" said Thelma.

"A human bean?" said James.

"A human being?" Roger said.

"Yes," said Harriet. "It saw me, too."

"Did it chase you?"

"Did it kick you?"

"Did it throw things at you?"

"No. It just stood and watched me flying. And its eyes got round, just like ours."

"Mother always said," Thelma remarked, thoughtfully, "that if you found the right kind of Hands, you'd never have to hunt again. But if you found the wrong kind, it would be worse than dogs, she said."

"I think this one is the right kind," said Harriet.

"What makes you think so?" Roger asked, sounding like their mother.

"Because it ran off and came back with a

plate full of dinner," Harriet said. "And it put the dinner down on that big stump at the edge of the field, the field where we scared the cows that day, you know. And then it went off quite a way, and sat down, and just watched me. So I flew over and ate the dinner. It was an interesting dinner. Like what we used to get in the alley, but fresher. And," said Harriet, sounding like their mother, "I'm going back there tomorrow and see what's on that stump."

"You just be careful, Harriet Tabby!" said Thelma, sounding even more like their mother.

CHAPTER 4

THE NEXT DAY, when Harriet went to the big stump at the edge of the cow pasture, flying low and cautiously, she found a tin pie-plate of meat scraps and kibbled catfood waiting for her. The girl from Overhill Farm was also waiting for her, sitting about twenty feet away from the stump, and holding very still. Susan Brown was her name, and she was eight years old. She watched Harriet fly out of the woods and hover like a fat hummingbird over the stump, then settle down, fold her wings neatly, and eat. Susan Brown held her breath. Her eyes grew round.

The next day, when Harriet and Roger flew cautiously out of the woods and hovered over the stump, Susan was sitting about

fifteen feet away, and beside her sat her twelve-year-old brother Hank. He had not believed a word she said about flying cats. Now his eyes were perfectly round, and he was holding his breath.

Harriet and Roger settled down to eat.

"You didn't say there were two of them," Hank whispered to his sister.

Harriet and Roger sat on the stump licking their whiskers clean.

"You didn't say there were two of them," Roger whispered to his sister.

"I didn't know!" both the sisters whispered back. "There was only one, yesterday. But they look nice—don't they?"

THE NEXT DAY, Hank and Susan put out two pie-tins of cat dinner on the stump, then went ten steps away, sat down in the grass, and waited.

Harriet flew boldly from the woods and alighted on the stump. Roger followed her. Then—"Oh, look!" Susan whispered—came Thelma, flying very slowly, with a disapproving expression on her face. And finally—"Oh, look, *look*!" Susan whispered—James, flying low and lame, flapped over to the stump, landed on it, and began to eat. He ate, and ate, and ate. He even growled once at Thelma, who moved to the other pie-tin.

The two children watched the four winged
cats.

Harriet, quite full, washed her face, and
watched the children.

Thelma finished a last tasty kibble, washed
her left front paw, and gazed at the children.

Suddenly she flew up from the stump and straight at them. They ducked as she went over. She flew right round both their heads and then back to the stump.

"Testing," she said to Harriet, James, and Roger.

"If she does it again, don't catch her," Hank said to Susan. "It'd scare her off."

"You think I'm *stupid*?" Susan hissed.

They sat still. The cats sat still. Cows ate grass nearby. The sun shone.

"Kitty," Susan said in a soft, high voice. "Kitty kit-kit-kit-kit-kit-cat, kitty-cat, kitty-wings, kittywings, catwings!"

Harriet jumped off the stump into the air, performed a cartwheel, and flew loop-the-loop over to Susan. She landed on Susan's shoulder and sat there, holding on tight and purring in Susan's ear.

"I will never never never ever catch you, or

cage you, or do anything to you you don't want me to do," Susan said to Harriet. "I promise. Hank, you promise too."

"Purr," said Harriet.

"I promise. And we'll never ever tell anybody else," Hank said, rather fiercely. "Ever! Because—you know how people are. If people saw them—"

"I promise," Susan said. She and Hank shook hands, promising.

Roger flew gracefully over and landed on Hank's shoulder.

"Purr," said Roger.

"They could live in the old barn," Susan said. "Nobody ever goes there but us. There's that dovecote up in the loft, with all those holes in the wall where the doves flew in and out."

"We can take hay up there and make them a place to sleep," Hank said.

"Purr," said Roger.

Very softly and gently Hank raised his hand and stroked Roger right between the wings.

"Oooh," said James, watching. He jumped down off the stump and came trotting over to the children. He sat down near Susan's shoes. Very softly and gently Susan reached down and scratched James under the chin and behind the ears.

"Purr," James said, and drooled a little on Susan's shoe.

"Oh, well!" said Thelma, having cleaned up the last of the cold roast beef. She arose in the air, flew over with great dignity, sat right down in Hank's lap, folded her wings, and said, "Purr, purr, purr..."

"Oh, Hank," Susan whispered, "their wings are furry."

"Oh, James," Harriet whispered, "their hands are kind."